KIDS CAN'T STOP READING THE *CHOOSE YOUR OWN ADVENTURE*™ STORIES!

"I like *Choose Your Own Adventure*™ books because they're full of surprises. I can't wait to read more."
—Cary Romanos, age 12

"Makes you think thoroughly before making a decision."
—Hassan Stevenson, age 11

"I read five different stories in one night and that's a record for me. The different endings are fun."
—Timmy Sullivan, age 9

"It's great fun! I like the idea of making my own decisions."
—Anthony Ziccardi, age 11

AND TEACHERS LIKE THIS SERIES, TOO!

"We have read and reread, worn thin, loved, loaned, bought for others, and donated to school libraries, the *Choose Your Own Adventure*™ books."

CHOOSE YOUR OWN ADVENTURE™— AND MAKE READING MORE FUN!

D0805048

Bantam Books in the Choose Your Own Adventure™ Series
Ask your bookseller for the books you have missed

SPACE AND BEYOND

R.A. MONTGOMERY

ILLUSTRATED BY PAUL GRANGER

BANTAM BOOKS
TORONTO · NEW YORK · LONDON · SYDNEY

RL 5, IL age 10 and up

SPACE AND BEYOND

A Bantam Book / January 1980

2nd printing . . . . . January 1980	5th printing . . . . September 1980
3rd printing. . . . . April 1980	6th printing . . . . March 1981
4th printing . . . . July 1980	7th printing . . . . July 1981

Dedicated to
ANSON & RAMSEY

<u>WARNING!!!!</u>

Do not read this book straight through from beginning to end! These pages contain many different adventures you can go on in space. From time to time as you read along, you will be asked to make a choice. Your choice may lead to success or disaster!

The adventures you take are a result of your choice. *You* are responsible because *you* choose! After you make your choice, follow the instructions to see what happens to you next.

Remember—you cannot go back! Think carefully before you make a move! One mistake can be your last . . . or it *may* lead you to fame and fortune!

You are born on a spaceship traveling between galaxies. The spaceship is on a research mission. The crew of the spaceship includes people from five different galaxies. Your parents are not from the same galaxy, but both have features common to those found on the planet Earth in the Milky Way galaxy.

Because you have been born in space *you* may choose which galaxy and planet you wish to belong to and have citizenship in.

Because the spaceship is traveling at a very great speed, you reach the earth-age of 18 years old in just three days and two hours. Now you must choose the planet *Phonon* in the galaxy of PINEUM or the planet *Zermacroyd* in the galaxy of OOPHOSS.

Phonon is three times the size of the planet Earth. The star that provides some of its life-giving force is huge but ancient. There is fear that it is losing its force. Phonon has a history filled with trouble.

Zermacroyd is in the galaxy OOPHOSS far distant from the Milky Way galaxy. This galaxy has black holes and supernova stars. It has always been regarded as an uncertain region by observers and spacecraft crews. It is a difficult area and the black holes are unplotted and dangerous. Reports from previous space probes say that Zermacroyd has had a dim and troubled past. The reports also prophesied a bright and exciting future.

*If you choose Phonon as your birth
planet, turn to page 2.*

*If, on the other hand, Zermacroyd
attracts you, throw your luck to page 3.*

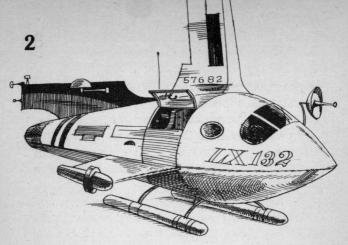

Phonon is visible on the galaxy scanner. Now that you have chosen, your parents announce that Phonon is your father's home. The crew of the spaceship carefully prepares a spacepod for the journey to Phonon. You seat yourself at the controls and position the programmed flight path, disengage from the mother ship and drift off into space. Once in space you are propelled by gravity generators.

Something is wrong! You look at the scanner and see a nebula that is not supposed to be on your course. Suddenly the gases and particles of the nebula surround you. Your gravity generators and life-support systems might fail. The radiation counter interrupts the silence of space flight with harsh bleeps and crackles a warning of dangerous radiation levels.

You can try to return to the mother ship. If you choose this, turn to page 4.

If you rely on and trust your instinct that says to go ahead, turn to page 6.

Zermacroyd! What a name. You can't resist this planet and its unknown past. When the captain mentioned the hope for a bright future, you decided that you must go there. It turns out that it is the home of your mother. She embraces you, wishes you luck, and gives you a small metal object on a chain.

"Perhaps this will help you some time."

Just as you are about to go for your final briefing, a young member of the flight crew rushes up and says, "Let me go with you. You will need my help." You don't know him well, but you have always found him warm and helpful. His name is Mermah, and his broad smile makes you feel happy about the adventures that lie ahead. Of course he can come.

The head of research warns you about Sun-Thee, a giant star twelve times the size of Earth's sun. Sun-Thee is in your path, and its enormous gravitational pull could be dangerous. He also cautions you about the black holes and supernovas. He tells you that if you want to delay your departure and go through the Space Academy, it may make your chances of success much better.

If you delay departure for further instruction, turn to page 7.

If you dash off, turn to page 8.

4

Return to the mother ship should be easy. You hit the navigation button and push the reverse command switch. But, just at that moment, the lighting in the pod turns to the flashing green/yellow warning color, and all systems stop. Swirling gas and dust particles bathe the pod. You frantically hit re-start buttons but nothing happens.

As suddenly as the gas came, it leaves. The warning lights go off, the control panel blinks with energy, and the navigation control systems say GO. The automatic S.O.S. signal turns off, and you sit exhausted in front of the controls.

If you decide to wait for help from the S.O.S. call, and then return to the mother ship, turn to page 10.

If you decide to go on now that the mysterious nebula has vanished, turn to page 11.

Heavy meteor showers interfere with your complex navigation system. The interference is so intense that all communications systems go out. You hurtle through space looking out through the portholes, amazed at the sights about you. But, your spacepod begins to tumble and the world spins in a maze of colors and shapes.

Your speed is so great that you should get through the shower soon, perhaps even soon enough to correct the navigational problems. On the other hand, maybe it is dangerous to assume that you can rely on chance to get you out of this fix. Wouldn't it be better and safer to radio for help? The laser radio will probably get through.

If you wait and hope to get through the shower, turn to page 12.

If you decide to radio for help, turn to page 14.

Hesitating, you ask what other types of instruction will be given to you. So far you have learned flight procedures, navigation, languages, weapons, and planning. It is a good idea to get as much information as possible, but you ask the head of research how you will know when you have learned enough.

"Knowledge is within all of us. You have but to realize it. Spend some time now. Then go."

"All right, I'll do as you suggest. But how long will it take?"

"You may either go to the Space Academy courses on board, or you may study with me and explore the knowledge within you." He does not smile, but he folds his arms to await your decision.

If you decide to attend the Space Academy, turn to page 15.

If you choose to explore the knowledge within yourself, turn to page 16.

You want to be on your way. Even though it might be a rash decision, you and your new companion Mermah climb aboard the spacepod. You enter the proper numbers on the flight panel and you launch into space.

"Mermah, check the stabilizers. We seem to be spinning a bit."

"OK. Will do."

Just then you realize from the computer screen that your flight path is close to a black hole. The danger is that once near the gravitational field of the black hole, you will never escape. Mermah helps you check the data input to the navigation system. To your dismay, you realize that instead of punching in the figures 4800, you actually put in

4008, and your path is now locked into the black hole.

Mermah stares at you in horror as the pod continues to move toward the massive black hole. People who have been trapped by black holes have never returned.

If you put on full power in hopes of breaking through the gravity field and landing on the black hole, turn to page 18.

If you put up the energy repulsion shields to try and escape the black hole, turn to page 19.

An S.O.S. sent in space is a risky thing. There is no telling who is out there. You wait with hope and a good measure of fear. Then you see it. First a speck on the screen moving in a sideways fashion. Then it jumps into focus. It resembles an amoeba, but it has lights, portholes, and markings of an unknown sort. Abruptly, the spacecraft—or whatever it is—halts close to you.

In space, alien beings are not uncommon. You are alien to the beings in this craft jiggling outside your spacepod. But, what should you assume? Are they hostile, or are they life forms knowing neither hostility nor friendship?

There isn't much time. You must decide whether to fight and hope you can drive them off, or whether you should just go quietly and peacefully with them. Here they come. It is hard to tell whether it is one or many. They seem to be all mixed together.

*If you decide to go willingly,
turn to page 20.*

*If you decide to fight,
turn to page 22.*

Your energy indicator has faded from full energy red light to one-quarter level blue-green light. Computer analysis warns you that all life support systems will stop in three hours, sixteen minutes. But, there has been no response to your S.O.S. Through your radar scan you realize that even if help does come, it will probably not reach you before all life support systems fail. You desperately wish that there were someone in the pod to share this with, but you are alone.

You have decided to use what remaining energy there is to follow a light/island message beaming from a black hole. Black holes in space are there because the mass of the star is so great that nothing can escape its gravity field—no light, no heat, no radio waves. Yet, mysteriously a light/island—a phenomenon talked about and recorded by a rare group of intergalactic pilots—is clearly indicated coming from the region of a black hole.

You must go. At least, you feel that the choice is either go toward the black hole and the light/island or drift in helplessness waiting for a chance rescue ship.

*If you choose the light/island,
turn to page 23.*

*If you choose to drift,
turn to page 26.*

Why wait? You just feel that you will make it through. You push the advance button, strap your seatbelts and shoulder harnesses even tighter, and push on. The bouncing and rocking is severe.

There is a popping sound. The spacepod is flung out of the meteor shower and into a transit zone.

The transit zone is a space highway designed for commercial use by transports. An amazing variety of spaceships are following different laser beam highways.

A transit zone patrol craft hovers near you and signals you to follow it. Stopping at a patrol station, you are informed that there is a space caravan that might stop at Phonon. Perhaps you could join it. It

is uncertain just when it will reach Phonon though, if ever. The alternative is a band of space entertainers, an interesting group who travel wherever they wish. You could join them. They too might stop at Phonon, but you never know.

If you go on the caravan.
turn to page 27.

If you become part of the show,
turn to page 24.

14

Trusting feelings works sometimes, but this situation is too dangerous. It's probably going to be embarrassing to ask for help so soon after starting out. You notice the palms of your hands and see the drops of sweat on them and their unusual whiteness. No question about it, you are scared—with good reason. Who wouldn't be?

"Spacepod, trans-galactic mission to planet Phonon, interrupted by meteor shower. System now three quarters inoperative. Repeat, Coordinate Z2380, F9212, X2922. Time reference. Outer Zone 2L. Request immediate aid. Repeat, request immediate aid."

Your voice feels small and hollow as it echoes in the pilot's compartment of the pod. You are so alone.

If you try the emergency booster engine to give you power to move forward in the direction of a faint radio signal, turn to page 28.

If you use the remaining power to increase your radio transmission, turn to page 29.

School can be boring, but then it might be just the thing for the flight. This space research vessel is so huge and so advanced that you didn't actually realize that there was a division of the Space Academy aboard. During your interview with the head of the Academy, he says, "Well, you choose. Either join Command School and become a captain of a ship, or go ahead and concentrate on research. We have done a personality, intelligence and health inventory on you, and you have scored very high. We believe you can make it to the top in either category. Well, what do you think?"

If you choose Command School turn to page 30.

If you choose to join the research program, turn to page 32.

16

The name of the head of research is Pherantz. He tells you that there is an infinity of knowledge stored within all living things from countless past experiences. It sounds crazy, but then you just can't tell. You wonder if you really can call on experiences from past lives. Are there flashes of memory locked in your cells? Are the dreams you have of places you have never been, things you have never done, people you do not know, actually experiences from a past life bubbling up within you looking for a way out? Maybe dreams are a real thing. You sense a feeling of calm in the philosopher.

"Remember my friend, all travel in space accomplishes little. We end where we begin. Parallel lines cross! Time is not real. Try to make the past the present."

Go on to the next page.

You feel uncomfortable with these heavy thoughts, especially when he talks about parallel lines crossing in space. What does infinity mean, anyway?

"We can experiment with the past." It is the philosopher talking again. "The past is not lost. It is just changed into a different form."

You spend days calling on past experiences. It is like a big dream machine.

"You are doing well. Would you like to give it a try?"

"What do you mean?" you ask.

"You can either travel now into past time—125 million Earth years ago, the age of dinosaurs, and wander around there—or you can just give it a chance and wander into an unknown past.

"Well, what is it?"

If you choose to go back in time 125 million years to the age of the dinosaurs, turn to page 33.

If you are willing to chance it and go back to an unknown past, turn to page 35.

18

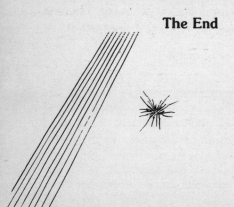

You are never heard from again. . . .

The End

"Don't give up! Try everything we can. Quick! Put up the energy repulsion shields."

It is Mermah talking. He is two years older and has traveled widely in space.

"What do you think will happen to us, Mermah?"

"One never knows," he replies.

With a shudder, the pod is suddenly grasped by the gravitational field, and you find yourself hurtling into a tunnel-like void. A black hole might seem black to the observer from outside because no light can possibly escape its gravitational field, but all the light and the energy is contained within this space. The tunnel is brilliantly lit but, strangely, the intense light does not hurt your eyes.

Then you are in a giant room. No, it is not a room, it is actually the interior of the black hole. It is a gigantic prism, thousands of miles across. It is a world unto itself. You are no longer frightened, and you and Mermah leave your spacepod to begin a life in a new world.

The new world is peaceful, and the people are friendly and eager to welcome you and Mermah. No one is in a hurry, and work is pleasant. There is food and housing for all. It's a good world.

The End

You don't know what these creatures are, and you realize your weapons might not work. It seems reasonable to meet them in an open and unarmed manner. They—or it—suddenly appear inside your own craft. You have heard of pure energy passing through solid matter and then reforming into its original shape. They call it dematerialization. But this catches you by surprise.

Part of the ship's equipment is a language/thought translation device designed to make contact between different life forms as easy as possible. This alien is certainly as different from you as anyone could possibly be. There seem to be hundreds of strange creatures around you one mo-

ment, then only one. The button on the device is close at hand, and you punch it immediately, announcing, "Welcome to my spacepod. I am on a mission to my own planet. I am peaceful."

The aliens do not respond. They make no noise, and suddenly they melt together into a large jumbled, jelly-like mass that surrounds you. You are caught in what feels like a slimy ooze. You try to kick free, but it is no use.

A sound emerges from the ooze. It is a combination of electronic beeps and lifelike bird calls. It does not reassure you. Then you feel a lightness that you have never before experienced, and in seconds you have been dematerialized and transported to the jiggling, free-form spacecraft that carries your captors.

Testing the substance their craft is made out of, you believe you could break through and escape. Their craft is wrapped around yours like Silly Putty on a tennis ball. All you need to do is figure out where your entrance hatch is, break through and get to the weapons you had stored on board. It is a slim chance, but a real one.

If you try to escape, turn to page 38.

If you go along without resistance, turn to page 36.

The creatures move toward your craft. Suddenly, there are more of them than you can count, in all different shapes and sizes. They invade your craft, where they seem to melt over the control board. The communications and navigation systems do not seem to be working. There is no other choice. You must fight for your life.

You reach for the emergency energy switch. Just as you do that, the creatures surrounding you melt together into a large jiggling form. With great difficulty you escape the sticky mass that holds you. A laser pistol is in your hand. You press the release button and aim at the center of the jiggling mass. You watch it shrivel, turn bright colors, smoulder, shudder, and *then* regenerate. You keep firing.

Sounds never before heard by humans fill the air. It is not music, and yet it has tone and a certain beauty to it. The more you fire the louder it gets. Unnoticed by you, the laser beams are hitting the instrument console, destroying major portions of it. You keep on firing. The mass shrivels, and vanishes. Silence. You have won.

But what a bitter victory. You now realize that the spacepod is destroyed. You float in space hoping for some chance rescue.

*To get another chance,
forget Phonon. Try Zermacroyd.
Turn to page 3.*

With all remaining energy resources, you propel the craft toward the black hole. The closer you get the more strange things happen to you. First, all the dials on the command console reverse and spin back to zero readings. Then your hair stands straight up as rigid as a wire brush. All light from your systems flows away in a stream and heads toward the black hole. You feel all your blood rush to your hands and feet, and a frightening dizziness overcomes you.

From one of the portholes, you see a pulsating, velvet-like mass larger than the sky—or so it seems.

A sharp, piercing cry wails, "Go back, before it is too late. Go back now."

You have absolutely no idea where this warning is coming from. Perhaps you can still turn back. Maybe it is not too late. Maybe there is enough energy reserve to escape the intense gravitational field of the black hole.

The warning is not repeated, and you hesitate about what to do next.

If you go on, turn to page 39.

If you try to reverse direction, turn to page 41.

You decide quickly. A space circus sounds crazy, but then the whole idea of wandering around galaxies looking for your home planet is crazy, too. You meet the leader, Ooxog, who can only be described as a totally normal looking earth-type with a red beard, a huge grin, the body of a giant, and a laugh and warmth that makes you feel at home.

"Welcome! We need a new thing. Welcome to the greatest show in the universe."

"But what can I do?"

"Don't worry, my friend. We will find you work. There is no problem there!"

So, you join this group of creatures, some earth-types, others like nothing you have ever seen. The array of odd spaceships hurtles through space, stopping at the odd planet or convenient space station, or just drifting in the void.

Your special job is to be the trainer of high energy particles and quarks, making them do tricks. You like quarks. And they seem to like you, too.

You never get to Phonon, but you no longer care.

The End

You did not expect to find black holes on your trip to Phonon. No preparation was given for this type of problem. True, you are bright and creative, but this problem facing you is too much. You can't risk the dangers of approaching the black hole.

You drift in space locked in an orbit just beyond the reach of the black hole. Watching your instruments, totally alone and desperate, you realize that time has stopped. All other equipment works, but no time is recorded. You check it all out, the clock seems fine. Then it hits you with full force.

Time doesn't exist out here in this void. Nor does space. Nor do *you*.

The End

A space caravan! What could be more exciting than wandering through the universe, going wherever chance takes you? A meeting is arranged with the leader of the space caravan. She is a beautiful Noomanian—beautiful at least by Noomanian standards. You communicate with her by using the language translation device.

Her name is Eus, and she explains to you that her group gathers exotic delicacies and objects. They never know where they are going. They go one stop at a time. For example, Eus informs you that they are on their way to the planet Earth with a consignment of black hole dust. The earthlings believe it is a magic potion giving them eternal youth. Eus laughs at that, saying, "Foolish earthlings, they always want what they can't have and what is really unimportant anyway." Then she says, "Come along, we can't wait."

So off you go. When you arrive on Earth, you are fascinated by this strange civilization with its tall ugly buildings, its people who look like you but are rushing, rushing, rushing and buying, buying, buying. It amuses you. What a peculiar place!

If you decide to stay on Earth, turn to page 42.

If you decide to leave, turn to page 43.

What luck. You are suddenly drawn by a tractor beam into the receiving bay of a giant mobile research station RS-3, UGB. It is under command of the Universe Governing Body and you are warmly welcomed by all aboard. They inform you that they are on their way to the planet Axle. It is a mercy mission, because this planet has been infected by a strange disease for which the Axlians know no cure. The research station could become infected, but that is the risk the scientists and doctors aboard are willing to take. What a dilemma! Out of the radar oven, and into the laser beam.

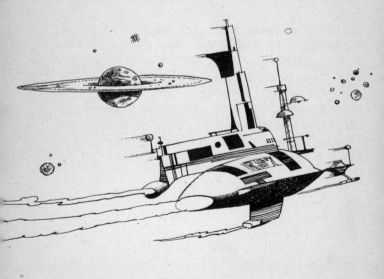

If you decide to go on to Axle with them,
turn to page 44.

If you choose to continue your journey
to Phonon, turn to page 45.

Your broadcasts for help interfere with a hostile forcefield, which amplifies your signal and returns it. Your entire spacepod is hit by a shock wave of your own amplified energy, and it explodes.

The End

Being a pilot-in-command of a space mission sounds impressive to you. You enroll in the Academy. Mermah decides to join you. All thought of going to either Phonon or Zermacroyd leaves you, as the courses of study interest you more and more each day. The time passes and you achieve advanced standing in the Academy. Your parents are proud of you, and upon graduation, you and Mermah are assigned to a new and radically different spacecraft designed to carry out deep probes into the remote and unexplored regions of intergalactic space.

Bidding all friends and family a farewell, you and Mermah enter the new craft for a twelve-year probe into uncharted regions.

The End

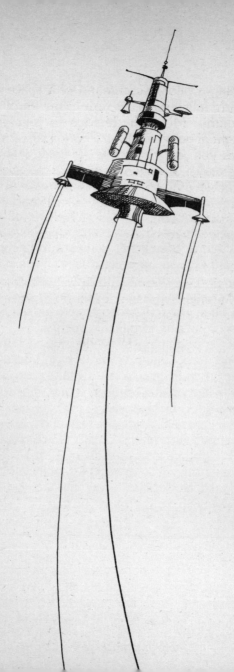

What is research about? You have heard nothing but "research, research, and more research" from everyone on the space station. It seems to you that research is just another name for messing around with whatever interests you. You'll give it a try.

"The subject of our research happens to be the cause of the violent trouble—specifically revolts—that occurs on *all* planets. Revolutions and wars have caused pain, but they have caused good things, too. What we want to find out is if the benefits can be gotten without the pain and horror of the uprisings." It is the research coordinator talking to a select group of six people. You have been chosen because of your aptitude for finding solutions to difficult puzzles.

This is beginning to really interest you. Your intention to journey to Phonon and Zermacroyd seems to fade into some distant place in your mind. Mermah has chosen to remain with you. He is a good companion.

After intensive work, the research team decides to split into two teams. Team A will head to the planet Cynthia to view a current revolt. Team B will join a mission exploring a revolt on Mars that happened 62 million years ago—a time transporter device will be used for that.

If you choose A, turn to page 46.

If you choose B, turn to page 49.

You remember studying the mind tapes of the evolution of living things on twelve planets. Earth was one of the planets, and the time period of the dinosaurs always fascinated you. The Cretaceous period when Tyrannosaurus Rex lived was a difficult but fascinating time. Suddenly, you are there, in a world without any human creatures. You are shocked to see that you have become a Velociraptor, very small in comparison to the Tyrannosaurus Rex and a prey to his voracious appetite.

Hiding behind some lush vegetation, you are frightened and hungry, but you don't dare move. Any movement in this world could end in a sudden and violent death. You hear a scuttling sound, and a small Protoceratops rushes by, saying, "It's all clear, now. Tyrannosaurus and that awful Tarbosaurus have gone off to quarrel by themselves. Maybe it will give us a break."

You cautiously peer out from the bushes and plants, then step gingerly away from your protective shelter. You gain a vantage point to watch Tyrannosaurus and Tarbosaurus locked in a bloody fight. You are horrified as their sharp teeth and powerful arms and legs tear at each other. There is a terrible howling roar of pain, then a crunching sound as Rex succeeds in biting off the head of his enemy.

Go on to the next page.

Then he turns his attention to the surrounding area and spots you. Crazed with blood lust, he races after you.

You had better get out while you can. You wildly hit some buttons on the time travel meter you carry in your claw.

If you hit the "Erase button,"
turn to page 48.

If you hit the "Time Return button,"
turn to page 50.

A chance to go to the unknown is probably really risky, but there is that desire in most people to take big risks. You race back in time toward the edge of eternity, the beginning of the entire universe. You achieve an elastic weightlessness, and a sense of complete peace and calm. There is no sound, no light. But no darkness either. You race back to the very beginning, to the pulsating, exciting start. You return *to the big bang* that started the whole thing. You are and you have been a part of everything, always. The beginning is the end.

The End

You act as natural as you can to help them understand that you are not a hostile person. These creatures of unknown origin seem to understand the body language of friendship. They reform again into a solid mass, and then they question you in a high, metallic voice. It reminds you of early tapes that had been found in the space museum of an old civilization on an unnamed planet. There is the same tinkly sound. This is what they said:

"We are half object, half life form. The line between living and non-living things is not clear where we come from, but then what is ever really clear?

"We need a creature like you to aid us in our trans-galactic search for a new planet. Our planet is in grave danger of atomic reorganization. We fear it will soon disintegrate. Our inability to remain in one way of being—object or life form—makes it necessary to join with a totally living creature. You have a choice. Help us in our search, or be cast adrift in this galaxy.

If you decide to join them in their search for help, turn to page 53.

If you refuse to go with them, turn to page 54.

Quick! There is no time to lose. Switch on the mind-scan computer and key into their thought patterns. The computer makes sounds almost like groans—it is too complicated a task to read the minds of these strange creatures.

Then it works. The mind-scan blinks, "Read-Out," ready for communication.

"Main energy source located in lower trident, sequential grid, negative factor 3, eliminate E34, B13, optimize radical paramater input and proceed with viable alternatives." It sounds like crazy Earth talk to you, but you follow it, and you realize that you can render these creatures helpless, and even destroy them if you wish.

"Listen to me. You have one chance. Either disengage from this assault or I will deactivate you. This is just a sample." You momentarily release the sequence programmed for deactivation. Within a microsecond the creatures begin to tremble. But they are tough.

If you think they will ignore your threat, turn to page 51.

If they negotiate, turn to page 52.

The light/island appears as a haven for you, and your spacepod comes to rest gently in the warm radiance. You leave the spacepod and are greeted by a group of six creatures who before your eyes change age and features, transforming from babies to old people. It is more than you can understand. It is frightening. It is watching the past become the present and the present turn into the future. It is a kaleidoscope of life, endlessly repeating the cycle of birth and death.

You realize that it is beginning to happen to you, as well. You look down at your hands and they are small and pink—baby's hands. Before your very eyes they grow and change color and texture. A rush of time and experience engulfs you. It is not unpleasant, but you have no control over it. Then, you are horrified to see the wrinkled skin and dark liver spots of old age appear on your hands.

Go on to the next page.

"Don't be too frightened," one of the creatures in front of you says. "All of us are shocked at the beginning, but it passes with time."

"What do you mean, it passes with time?" you shout.

They laugh, but not unkindly, and you calm down.

"Look, here. You must accept the fact that you now belong either to the past or the future. The present doesn't really exist. Why not choose where you would like to spend time? Oh, dear, as we said, there is no time, really. But don't worry. Past or future, it's up to you."

If you will risk going into the future, turn to page 55.

If you want the comfort of the past, turn to page 56.

Hitting reverse engine and power output buttons frantically, you feel the spacepod tumble wildly as if out of control. Then there is a period of calm, quickly followed by more tumbling.

Then you are awake, wide awake. You glance at the control console, check the graph, navigational computer, and realize that you are on the route to Phonon, that all is well, that you had simply passed into a programmed sleep period which had produced the dreams of nebulae showers, light/ islands, and black holes.

On you go toward Phonon.

The End

42

Earth fascinates you. You have heard many stories about its history—a history of violence, of wars, of great destruction and hatreds that smouldered for years and even generations. It is described as one of the more hostile worlds, and only real adventurers risk spending much time there. Then there are those earth people who, in spite of all the violence, designed great societies benefiting all earthlings. It certainly is a mixed picture. Maybe you should stay.

So, you transfer to earth life systems by programming your bio-computer to accommodate for earth atmosphere, language and food intake.

You find earth types open and friendly, but you recognize an air of suspicion among them.

If you stay, turn to page 57.

If you leave, turn to page 58.

When you land on the planet Earth, the pilot of the second largest spacecraft picks a fight with you. He says, "Listen, you don't belong with us. We don't want you around. You stay here or I'll vaporize you."

He waves a laser pistol around. You have no idea why he is so angry, but there is no sense in taking risks. You'll stay on Earth for some time, and let them leave. But eventually you will have to set out again. Maybe a different route this time. Perhaps your new route will take you closer to Zermacroyd.

Turn to page 3.

RS-3, UGB enters the atmosphere of Axle. The scientists anxiously scan the operating equipment that monitors atmospheric conditions, existence of microorganisms, and energy relations. All seems natural. The ship hovers above the major city, Ntial. A landing party is formed. You are not asked to join, but you are fascinated by what is happening below. The TV monitors reveal a city in silence. Few living beings are seen, and those that are found look weak and listless.

The landing party radios back that a strange fever has gripped Axle, affecting virtually all its inhabitants. They are too weak to help themselves.

The research landing party now reports that three of its members are exhibiting symptoms similar to the Axlians'. They are retreating to formulate new plans. They also report that obviously certain beings from other planets are immune while others are not. They feel that only the immune should work on the planet to help fight the disease.

If you think you are immune, turn to page 59.

If not, turn to page 61.

You assess the dangers of traveling to a planet infected with a strange disease. You decide that you are not equipped to handle the problems. After a long, honest talk with the ship's commander, he says, "I understand your reluctance to join us, and I commend you for your courage in admitting your fear and concern. We will do what we can to help you on your way. Good luck. Gleeb Fogo (the Universal Salute of Friendship)."

Your spacepod is now repaired and outfitted for the journey. You are catapulted away from the research station, returning to the black void, spinning, spinning into the comfort of energy, timelessness, and endless space.

Turn to page 62.

Swirling clouds, dense with a moisture much heavier than water, cover the planet of Cynthia. Your spacecraft penetrates these clouds and bursts out onto a landscape of rich vegetation. No towns or cities are visible as the craft flies over the empty landscape. Where are the people? Where is the revolt?

You land with the advance party, and find the atmosphere almost acceptable to your bio-system.

You need only the smallest assistance from the life support pack. Mermah accompanies you.

"Did you see that?"

"What? What did you see?"

"Only a shadow. A shadow moving quickly, as though it were following us."

Then a short blast of a hornlike device stops you in your tracks. You are surrounded by flickering shapes, living creatures who blend and twist like shadows. You can't tell what they are.

"Peace or war? You! Are you the leader or just the follower?" It's the shadow people speaking.

"Peace, of course. In our world we don't believe in war."

"They all say that, but the wars rage throughout the entire universe."

"What are you people doing? Why did you ask for help?"

"We are fighting the forces of light, who are our enemies. We are the shadows."

You don't know whether to believe them or not, but there is no choice. You must go with them. They take you to headquarters. There they explain how the forces of light have attempted to wipe out the shadow people by creating a world with no shadows where light comes from all directions. The light people will not allow the mix of light and dark that colors life.

If you and Mermah join the forces that will fight on land, turn to page 65.

If you sign up with the rocket ship crew, turn to page 66.

You flee just in time to escape the brute. However the erase button you hit doesn't really lead to anywhere or anytime. You radio for help and direction.

Suddenly you are back in a spacepod, headed for Phonon. Oh, no, it's beginning all over again. You can't stand it.

Turn to page 2.

Time travel is frightening. When you rush back in time, it is like riding a roller coaster backward, only faster. You can watch the universe through your private porthole. You see stars born and see them die, you see planets spin off into space, comets come and go, supernovas exploding, and all the time, you are not even there. You are but pure energy counting down in time until you stop at Mars, a planet of a small sun in the Milky Way galaxy—an almost unheard of planet in an insignificant galaxy.

When you arrive on Mars, you are invisible and can travel through space, through solid matter, and even into the thoughts of people.

What is the cause of revolt on Mars? Who knows. Greed? Famine? Envy? Jealousy? Maybe just an instinctive need to battle, a basic drive to test and fight for the sheer sense of fighting. It's too complex. Everyone has a different answer. They all point to the other guy. All you know is that creatures get killed, cities get destroyed. What a way to live. That's why there is a new way—if only it will work. You are part of the new way, a way of sharing.

The End

50

The buttons on your time travel meter catapult you through space time to the Eastern part of Africa now called the Olduvai Gorge, in the Great Rift Valley. Only when you get there, it is not a gorge, nor is it a rift valley. It is an upland plain. It is four million years ago in Earth time. It is the dawn of mankind, and the earliest human types are just developing their life patterns. They live as hunters and gatherers. They have discovered tools, and they have begun to use objects like sticks and animal bones as weapons. It is the beginning of civilization. Why not hang around and see what happens? Maybe you can change it all.

The End

Ignoring you is their biggest mistake. They thought you were bluffing, but of course you weren't. Not with your life at stake!

You program the proper codes and watch these hostile, doubting creatures begin to vanish in just microseconds. You feel a sublime satisfaction, a supreme power; and then you begin to realize that something is happening to you. Something that is unbelievable!

If you continue to destroy the hostile creatures, turn to page 67.

If you just want to disable them and take command, turn to page 68.

52

They are impressed with the demonstration you have just put on. Drawing together in a loose, jumbled mass, they murmur and burble for several moments. Then a part of the mass seems to separate, draws itself into a close approximation of a human form and announces in a high-pitched singsong voice, "We recognize that you may have the power to destroy us. But we have decided to trust you. If you were hostile, you would have destroyed us without thinking twice. We believe that you are good." There is a burble of assent from the jumbled mass. The speech continues.

"We are on a mission from our home planet. We desperately need a special plasma that provides the energy for our thought generators. Without this plasma, which is no longer available on our planet, we are finished. We will become just big, messy blobs without direction. We need the guidance of thought. It is known that the plasma is available on two planets. One of them has the name Phonon."

You almost jump out of your skin.

"Wow! Right on!" you quip. "Let's go."

Then, everything seems to stop. A strange sound permeates the void. It is neither loud nor soft, but it is obvious that it is completely outside all of you.

*If you think the sound is friendly,
turn to page 69.*

If not, turn to page 70.

Part of their team is in search of the vital energy plasma needed to help them think. But the main group is on a mission to collect samples of other life forms from a wide variety of planets. They hope to gain enough information from the many different types of life to aid them in the development of their change from object to life form. They mention that this "research" would be of great help to all beings in the trans-galactic universe.

You realize that you are one of their specimens and that frightens you. They propose that you join them in this mission. Since their form is so repulsive, they need someone like you to lead the advance scouting parties for life form collection. You will be their lure! You don't like the idea, but they promise that no harm will come to any of the collected life forms. After study and evaluation, they will be returned to their original homes. What have you got to lose? You might as well go along. It could be interesting.

They present you with two missions. The first is to travel to a planet with earth-type creatures, the second is to penetrate a small, diminishing star searching for object-life.

If you choose the mission to an earth-type planet, turn to page 72.

If you are attracted to the risks of investigating a small star, turn to page 73.

No, you don't want any part of these weirdos. Go ahead, cast adrift. You would prefer to be on your own. But, when they cast you adrift, they warn you that your lack of care can only provide trouble for you in the future. In a way, they have put a curse on you for your lack of caring. But, they started it all.

If you seek revenge, turn to page 74.

If you pay no attention to their words, turn to page 75.

Future! Throughout all time (if there is any such thing as time) creatures have wanted to be able to predict the future. Sometimes they consult gods or goddesses. Sometimes they even cut open animals, to search for the truth. Sometimes they go into trances, but most often they just hope that luck will help them tell what the future will bring. Nothing ever seems to really work. But now, you can travel into the future.

"Step this way, you must be prepared for this futuristic trip." They lead you up a long ramp surrounded on all sides by constantly changing light and images.

"Now, be quiet, remain calm, and enjoy!"

Suddenly, you leap into the future.

If you believe in the future,
turn to page 76.

If you doubt what's going on,
turn to page 77.

56

Returning to the past you believe is the safest and probably the most interesting thing to do. But what does the past mean? Five minutes ago, a year, three hundred years, two million? It's too general. You have to choose a specific time in the past, or if not a time, then a period.

If you choose to see the universe two billion years ago, turn to page 78.

If you want to see the past one hundred years, turn to page 79.

What an interesting planet. There are many different people, languages and customs. You could travel and learn so much on this small planet. True, there are grave problems, like pollution, wars, and the energy crisis. But you believe that progress is being made. The large political group called the United Nations is trying to solve some of the problems. People are tired of the wars. Yes, you decide that Earth is a worthwhile place to stay. Maybe you can help make it a better place to live.

The End

The video discs on the spaceship had shown pictures of the problems on Earth. There were problems of too many people, too little food, too much crime, pollution. Now that you are actually on Earth, you realize that those problems are real. It frightens you. Where do you start to solve these problems? What can be done? But it is too late, you can't leave the planet. An enormous tremor shakes the ground. Earthquakes and tidal waves destroy cities. The cause is unknown, but people suspect that several nuclear explosions were at fault.

The End

You *are* immune to this strange disease on Axle. The doctors and scientists confirm that your biochemical makeup will not be affected by the fever below. Down you go in a small transporter with three other immune members of the crew.

"Weird, isn't it?"

"Yeah. It's like the whole city is dead. Look at that guy over there. Why, he's barely able to walk."

"Like I said, it's weird."

"There has to be a cause for it, though. I mean, it's affecting everyone."

Your team interviews several of the sick people they come upon. All tell the same story of a sudden onset of sickness. In a matter of days, the entire population was immobilized. They did not notice any real changes before the start of the disease. The only different event was a visit by delegates from another planet, who were searching for some escaped politicians. Then nothing, only the sickness.

Go on to the next page.

You question them about these delegates from another planet, but the answers are vague and uncertain. They can't remember the name of the planet. They can't recall the serial numbers of the spaceship. They are of little help. Perhaps these delegates were hostile and had a plan for Axle.

Other people you interview talk of the warnings of a small group of scientists that pollution on their planet would soon cause them troubles that they would not be able to handle. They too are vague and uncertain.

If you go in search of the delegates, turn to page 80.

If you search for the sources of pollution, turn to page 82.

You are taken ill with the strange fever. One by one, the other crew members become infected with the fever. Even those who were supposed to be immune are not. The spaceship commander is out of his mind with the pain of the fever, and he tries to escape by going to another planet.

"We've got to escape. We have to go elsewhere," he shouts as the ship screeches away from Axle. But you might be carrying the fever wherever you go. After several weeks of aimless wandering, the Universe Governing Body sends out pursuit ships to capture you.

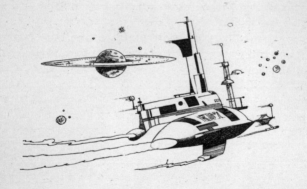

If you devise a plan before you are captured, turn to page 84.

If you conduct a computer search for the cause of the disease, turn to page 83.

Suddenly you are in the midst of laser beam shots. Your optical scanner shows eleven space-crafts. Four bear the design of Lodzot, and six have the look of Marly about them. The eleventh ship seems to be a Universe Governing Body police craft.

Whammo! The laser beam hits the Universe Governing Body police ship. It explodes into a million bright, shining patterns, but one of the Lodzot ships breaks off to investigate you!

"Come to a complete stop! Deactivate laser cannon. Identify yourself." It is the Lodzot ship commander.

"OK, OK, keep your hat on. I'm friendly." It's you speaking.

"Friendship comes in many forms. We have heard those words before. Will you join us against our enemy?"

If you don't join them in their fight, you are vaporized. It is . . .

The End

BUT

If you join them, turn to page 64.

So you join them. But you feel forced into a conflict that apparently has no meaning. They can't tell you why they are fighting. They were ordered to, so they do it. It makes no sense.

The other ships have come to a defensive formation and radio for a truce. You offer to be the negotiator. There is a mumbled conversation between spaceship captains, and then they say, "Tell us why we should negotiate."

"What's the use in fighting? You'll all get killed. No one wins."

"We'll talk it over." It's the Lodzot commander.

*If you stay on as negotiator,
turn to page 87.*

*If you make a run for it,
turn to page 86.*

Mermah convinces you to join up with the land forces in defense against the light people. You and Mermah are put in command of a group of 14 shadow battalions, and you build a system of walls to block the light sources. The tension builds as the light people send messages demanding surrender of the shadow forces.

A council is held, and you and Mermah are invited to attend.

"Shall we attack them, or shall we retreat? We can't possibly defend ourselves against them."

You and Mermah confer with the shadow forces.

If you decide to attack,
turn to page 88.

If you retreat, turn to page 89.

The rocket ship forces sound the most interesting, and besides, you are trained as a space pilot. Ground forces would be difficult for you. You are promoted to a command rank and put in charge of a large spacecraft with laser rocket weapons. From then on you are in space searching out and destroying alien ships.

But you think to yourself, is this any kind of life, forever destroying things? Maybe you will quit.

The End

Whap! Zork! Squarsh! They or it or whatever lies quivering in a sodden and then crispy mass on the cabin floor. But, the energy charge was so great, you too are transformed from your present form into pure energy. Maybe you can start all over. Maybe you can rematerialize. Try it.

If you try to rematerialize and go to Phonon, turn to page 2.

So, now you are in command. Does that feel good? No? Lonely perhaps? No? Confusing? Well, being in command probably feels like all those things. It's in your hands. Get on with it.

First you will search their memory banks, check ships' logs for previous missions, and put all the data together for an answer. It's confusing, but you persist.

Like a puzzle in three dimensions, the data form an incomplete picture of a planet in the midstage of evolution from objects with the beginning of consciousness to true life forms. Somewhere things got crossed and these half-object/half-living creatures launched themselves bodily into space, searching for thoughtfulness. They believed this thoughtfulness would solve their problems.

The End

The sound increases in intensity. It actually changes in pitch and suddenly the energy in the sound transforms into light. The entire area is bathed in beautiful colors that radiate warmth and positive force. The light seems to unify everything around you. There is a strong pleasant feeling, and then there is a quick pulsation, and you jump into hyper-space with a rush almost unbelievable in its intensity. The light serves as the vehicle carrying you and these other creatures on a journey toward an unknown place.

If you try to break the light vehicle's hold on you and return to your craft, turn to page 97.

If you go on, turn to page 98.

Where is the sound coming from? Then a huge shadow reaches over you. All systems stop. There is a humming sound and it fills the space. Looking up you see a giant spacecraft, larger than anything you have ever seen or heard about. It glows with a soft greenish light and the humming sound is obviously coming from it.

A transport beam picks you up, and suddenly you are inside the giant spacecraft. Oddly, no one or nothing with life seems to be aboard this craft.

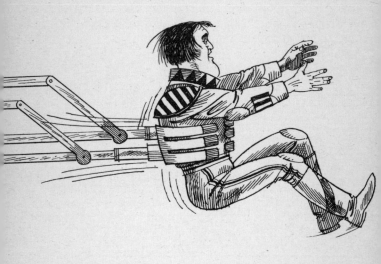

You are placed by means of mechanical arms in a small room. Food, books, music, tapes are on a table. The humming stops. Then a voice says, "We have been searching for you, and we welcome you to life aboard Craabox. We are a small world of ourselves. We need your type to complete our society. Enjoy yourself. No harm will come to you."

The humming sounds begin again, and you doze off into deep sleep.

When you awake, you are told by the voice to go either to room 99 or 100. You ask why, but the voice only says choose. Choose what? It's a flip of the coin—there is no real choice. Go ahead, flip.

If you choose room 99,
turn to page 99.

If you flip and choose 100,
turn to page 100.

"We approach planet Orgone from a direction which keeps us in the shadow of its moon. We will land in an unpopulated area and proceed with specimen gathering." It is their minimum leader talking. The maximum leader has been ordered to return for very high, very important, very complicated, unknown negotiations back at their base. Maybe a minimum leader is a better thing. At any rate, down you go, and make a landing in a sandy area covered with small bushes.

"Nobody or nothing here all right," you report as the first one to step out of your craft.

"Proceed with gathering plan." It is the minimum leader speaking.

Making your way into a small town, you are amazed at the life forms. They are like you, but they all talk too fast. They are in a feeding frenzy, putting round discs into their mouths. They are pouring brown liquid after the round discs. There is strange sound coming from brightly colored boxes. It is all very strange indeed. Everything is done quickly. You feel uncomfortable.

Then an idea pops into your brain. "Maybe I can escape. I look like them, maybe I'll just join them and run away." You join a line to receive the discs and the brown fluid (some of the fluid is orange, white, brown—yuck).

If you continue your escape,
turn to page 90.

If not, turn to page 91.

Stars are masses of extremely hot gases which emit energy in the form of exploding atomic particles. The violence of their continual nuclear reactions is unbelievable. Why in the world would you want to go on a mission to penetrate such a world? But that is what you have chosen to do.

The group you have joined is enthusiastic about this mission. They know that if they are successful in penetrating this particular sun and returning with samples of object-life, that they will become Seoreh (heroes) in their land. Anything for fame.

The spacecraft enters into a wide orbit about this sun, and then at the proper moment, with all heat deflection shields, antimatter reflectors, and dematerialization gear operative, it breaks orbit and dashes for the sun. It is sheer madness, and you realize it much too late to do anything about it. You are transformed into basic energy particles.

The End

Space is enormous and thoughts of revenge fade. By sheer luck you intersect a course set by a band of other spacecraft that are renegades from Earth, Acxr, X321, Mowon, and 0000. Communications with them are not difficult. It is not clear whether these renegades are actually space pirates or just adventurous wanderers. After many hours of talk explaining what happened to you, the new friends propose one of two missions.

If you form a battlegroup with them and search for the ship and its creatures that caused you trouble, turn to page 92.

If you forget the past, and forge ahead with them as space adventurers (read pirates if you wish), turn to page 93.

Get away as fast as you can. Yuck, what a group! It is so comforting to be in command of your own ship again. In a moment of pure joy at your release from the alien creatures, you over-program the velocity control, and with a swoosh you accelerate beyond the VNE (velocity not to exceed) mark.

You keep accelerating, and there seems to be no end to your speed. Things begin to blur. The outline of the control console becomes indistinct. The lights seem to brighten, and you recognize that there is no barrier between you and outer space. You merge into starry emptiness.

The End

In an enormous, dimly lit room, a small light rests on a table. You know that you must go to the table. There is a faint smell of sagebrush (a plant found on some deserts on the planet Earth). A voice instructs you to open a book on the table. There is no book, and then it appears. It is a history

of your past lives for 6 million years. You are staggered by the great number of lives you have lived—sea captain, space pilot, wife of a slave, king. You have been poor and rich, married to beautiful women, plain women, nice ones, kind ones, and others. You have been a success and a failure, many times over. You have been happy and miserable. Only twice in all that time were you bored.

"Hey, wait a minute, I thought I was going into the future. That's what I agreed to, you guys. Come on now. An agreement's an agreement."

"The past is also the future. You have much to learn. Look to what you have learned. Then the future will reveal itself."

The End

It's just a lot of talk. You have heard this tale before. You can't waste your time on them.

Maybe you can find your way back out of this crazy mess. Past and future the same! Bunk!

But there is no way out—at least it appears that way.

The End

Two billion years ago. You can't even conceive of two billion as a number. What is it? Then you are there. Clouds of particles fill to void. Stars appear, planets burst forth, blackness is turned aside by the light from millions of stars. You wander in a mist of light and small particles. It is beautiful.

The End

OK, if you are going to see only the past 100 years, where do you want to see them? On Earth? That's a funny choice. Why not somewhere else? You just want to see Earth. It's up to you, so let's go.

Earth over the last hundred years: population explosion, overcrowded cities, progress from horses to spacecraft. Artificial limbs and heart operations. Giant farms run by machines. Oil discovered and then used up. Great wealth, great poverty. Rapid change. Where will it end?

If you choose to watch the future,
turn to page 109.

If you want to go elsewhere,
turn to page 110.

It is possible that hostile aliens infected Axle for a purpose. Your team reports back and is assigned a search mission to find the delegates and track down what they were doing.

Only one clue exists. It is a radio transmission recorded on your research vessel when Axle made its call for help. The message is unclear, but it gives space coordinates that include the neighboring planet of Fleedes. You travel there, and what you find is appalling. The planet is almost uninhabited. There is the wreckage of cities and towns. It looks like a massive war has taken place, but there is no

evidence of a victorious force in command. There is evidence of the fever here too.

*If you choose to
conduct a cleansing operation,
turn to page 111.*

*If you decide to search
the past to find cause of the plague
or whatever is ruining
this civilization, turn to page 112.*

82

Pollution of the air, the water, the land happened quickly on Axle. Your research shows that in just three generations the air became almost unbreathable and the water unfit to drink. Little care or attention was given to what was going on, and the toxic levels built up quickly. While the leaders argued about solutions, the people waited for things to get better. Then the fever started taking hold. You find out that the fever was caused by a combination of pollutants and the general decline of health in the population.

You can try to get the remaining Axlians to make changes to stop pollution. If so, turn to page 113.

If you feel that this is a problem for the Galactic Court, turn to page 114.

The histories of all worlds include sad stories of plagues and fevers and diseases and epidemics. But the worst of all these is the sickness brought on by excessive exposure to radiation. And you never checked on Axle to see if their nuclear reactors were emitting dangerous radiation levels. It's so simple, so obvious. People get careless, times get lax, accidents happen. This fever isn't caused by a bacteria. It's radiation sickness of the worst kind. There is no cure.

The End

84

The pursuit ships follow a trail of infectious fevers left behind on several planets, marking your mad dash to escape. Soon the word is out, and protective shield devices prevent your crew from entering the atmosphere of any planet. Three of your crew die of the fever, but you seem to be getting no worse, and you might even be getting better. Then you propose a startling idea.

"Look, let's go back to Axle where the fever started. We can only find the cure at the start."

Reluctantly the remaining crew members agree, and you head back to Axle. They take your advice because you have shown courage and wisdom under stress.

If you really believe that you can find the cure, turn to page 116.

If you don't really think that anything can be done, turn to page 115.

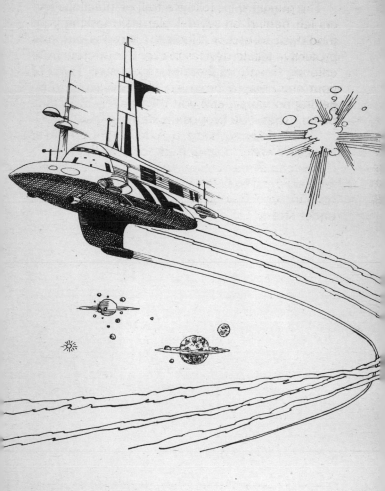

86

Make a run for it! It's foolish to stay in the middle of this fight. Who cares what they are fighting about. You push the maximum acceleration button and leave the area.

Laser cannon shots follow your path but the computer-directed evasion tactics enable you to escape.

Finally you are back alone in space.

The End

No one really wants to fight. Too many have been killed already. You negotiate a peace between the opposing forces. They are all that is left of a great armada of spaceships who have been fighting for more than three thousand galactic years. They are the last survivors. They have even forgotten the original cause of the war.

The End

Planet Cynthia has become a battlefield. Everything is being destroyed. Smoke hangs over the cities. Wreckage clutters the land. Your group attacks with laser weapons, but the enemy forces seem too strong to hold off. Your troops are being killed; everything is in shambles.

If you can hold off the enemy until you escape, turn to page 94.

If you give up, turn to page 96.

Retreat is not always a bad thing. After all, you should go with what feels right. To fight now would only create further destruction. Enough damage has been done. Level off, give way. Let the other side realize what has been happening, too.

As you retreat, the enemy seems to let up in amazement. The smoke clears, the noise stops. They retreat also. There is no more fighting.

The End

Escape seems easy. You gag when you try to put one of the discs in the hole you have in your head. It feels funny and is covered with a yellow gummy layer and on top of that is red ooze and small round green discs. What strange food.

You blend in with the others. They don't take much notice of you, because they are so busy with themselves. The noise from the colored boxes is deafening to your sensing devices. You move off with a crowd of them. Imitating them, you crumple up paper and throw it around. What strange customs.

Outside you get in a big vehicle painted a dull green. Someone shouts at you. The vehicle starts up, and you are driven off to a large camp outside the town. It says on a big sign, "Welcome to the Army." You are not sure, but you think you have just joined a military group.

If you choose to stay and find out what's going on, turn to page 101.

You have one secret weapon left that you have not used. If you choose to use it turn to page 106.

Escape will just lead to recapture. You might as well just go along with the mission. With a cheap bravery born of the knowledge that nothing can hurt you on Earth, you capture what earthlings call a politician (very dangerous creature), a student (also dangerous) and a government worker (unknown whether dangerous or not). They all look alike. Your mind-scan computer says that they all think alike, basically. At least, they all started out with the same opinions.

Along the way, you stop to enjoy the view, but it is quickly covered up with thick gray smoke from millions of small boxes with discs that race along gray ribbons.

*If you question the student,
turn to page 102.*

*If you question the politician,
turn to page 105.*

Forming a triangular force group of spacecrafts, you accelerate to maximum speed and search the immediate galactic space for the odd spacecraft and its inhabitants. The scanning devices of all ships are tuned to the wrong frequency. You realize that these creatures will not give off life-type response signals, nor will their craft respond in the normal fashion to radar probes. The craft is a soft, gelatinous mass, capable of absorbing the energy of the radar probe and storing that energy for its own use. Any radar probe will not bounce back to your screens. It will simply be lost.

Then you see it, just by the luck of your intuition. It lies directly ahead. The triangle battle group forms, slows, and concentrates its multiple power on the odd craft. With a gulping slurch the strange ship erupts and dematerializes.

Well done? You aren't really sure.

The End

"Forget them, brother. They have nothing we need. Revenge is a tiresome process." It is the space commander. She is speaking in a gentle tone.

"Well, what do we do now?" You always need a plan.

"We are going on a search mission. You see, my new friend, we tend to find things we need on other planets. We simply take them, whenever we can. We try and hurt no one, but there are risks."

"Why, you are pirates! Do you think I would ever join you in this madness? What about the Universe Governing Body?"

There is a chuckle from several of the space pilots, but you can't tell whether they are laughing at you, or just at the idea of the Universe Governing Body.

What a mess. What do you do now? You just don't know.

Flip a coin and see what happens.

If it comes up heads, turn to page 107.

If it comes up tails, turn to page 108.

There is a chance to get away. During a quiet moment, your group escapes to some remote hills far away from the battle area. Then something happens. The energy source for the lasers, the spacecrafts, the communications systems, mysteriously vanishes. There is no more energy except your own human energy. Weapons are useless. Radios and transports are just pieces of metal and plastic. They are not working either. To survive now, you will have to hunt for food and support each other.

The End

Surrender! But, if you don't give in, everything will be destroyed. What does surrender mean? You are frightened, but history has often shown that the conquerors don't often remain conquerors. They become a part of a new civilization with qualities from both the vanquished and the victors. But still, giving up is a last resort.

After long talks with your group, you all decide to take the risk of surrendering, and joining up with the conquerors. It is done.

The End

After all the trouble, both you and they realize that sharing—even though that seems impossible—is probably the only way. Too much is lost in the fighting. The Universe Governing Body has always tried to promote sharing, but it seldom works. Here is the chance. Now is the time. You join sides to promote the sharing of energy throughout the galaxies.

The End

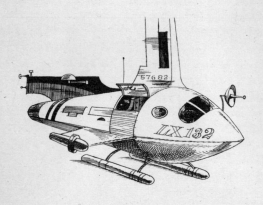

The Universe Governing Body has serious news. There is a major energy drain throughout all galaxies. No one has been able to identify the cause of the loss of energy, but there is a shutting down of systems in all quadrants; transportation, communication, life support, *all* systems. It is as though a giant battery were drained and growing weaker by the minute. You are all on your own now.

The End

Well, well, so your flip landed you here. What a surprise, your luck has just reversed time and space. You are back at the start. You have been given another chance. Try again! And good luck!

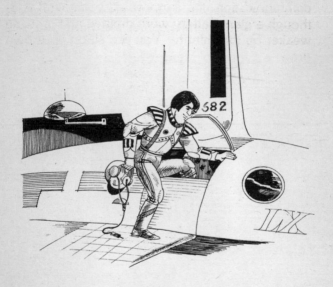

Turn to page 1.

Not bad. You flipped and you won. Room 100 is the Chamber of Leadership. You will be made commander of this strange artificial world. You will learn all that is to be learned, you will see all there is to see, you will then guide this roving mini-world through the galaxies investigating, learning more, collecting specimens of other life forms.

The End

Wherever you go, people or creatures seem to be fighting. They want more land, or water, or power, or maybe just excitement.

You become a natural leader, because the forces you join are leaderless and tired of conflict. After listening to all the complaints, you offer to negotiate for peace. But at your first negotiation with the hostile forces, you are captured and the war goes on.

The End

"OK, student, tell me about yourself. What is a student, anyway?"

The student is relaxed. At least he is out of school, and he isn't really afraid of you.

"Well, I don't know. Being a student is like being a prisoner. Everyone is always telling you what to do, where to go, what not to say, and you always get yelled at. It's a bummer."

You are shocked by what he says. After all, you enjoyed learning things. You ask, "Isn't there anything good about being a student?"

"Well, vacations, and you don't usually have to do much. You can get by."

"Are you dangerous?" you ask.

"No, they only think so. We aren't."

Suddenly the student leaps up and grabs you by the arms. You are tied up. Now you are his prisoner. He says, "See how you like it. I'm calling the authorities."

He makes the call, and soon you are carried away by uniformed men. You will be the object of study for years to come. Your freedom is gone forever.

The End

104

"A politician, what is that?" you ask.

The person hems and haws. Then the person begins to speak. "A politician serves the people and helps them make the right choices. We are very, very, very IMPORTANT! Why, without us there would be no *problems*—I, I mean, without us, problems would not appear to be so large. I—I—mean, well, I mean we create more problems than we solve and that is how we stay in office because someone has to solve them."

The politician begins to smile. He acts very friendly and says, "Hey, wait a minute. You're from another planet. We could become famous, you and I. Think of it. The whole world will want to see you and hear all about it. I'll be your manager. We'll make a bundle!"

You get out of there as fast as you can. You want no part of this freak show. But as you try to leave, he blocks the way, and you are caught. You remain on Earth as a curiosity from outer space.

The End

You remember a secret weapon given to you before you left the research ship. It is an intergalactic slow-time weapon. When you operate it, all motion and action freezes in time. No one is hurt, and the simple release of the energy field restores motion. You activate the device and disarm all the people on both sides. Then you program a future time leap to a place in time when peace is possible. It is weird wandering around with all these people looking like statues, but then suddenly they are alive again and wonder at the new world. They actually have forgotten the past and they can start again.

The End

Pirates in all ages and places have taken whatever they could grab. It makes no difference whether they are pirating sailing ships, or airplanes, or spacecrafts. Pirates live outside society; they must be banished.

You and your group of pirates are surrounded by Universe Governing Body pursuit ships. You are deported to a distant and dim galaxy and guarded by Universe troops. Your pirating days are over.

The End

What fun to be a pirate! It is a good life, and the treasure box on the spacecraft overflows with Universe Governing Body money.

But then, one day, you intercept a radio broadcast. The Universe Governing Body announces that all currency and money are worthless and no longer needed or used. A new system for sharing food, clothing, and shelter that doesn't use money has been set in motion. As pirates you are finished. There is nothing left to steal.

The End

The future of life on Earth is almost too much to think about. Anything could happen. You give it a try. Selecting the future in fifty years, you find yourself with a group of about sixty people, all young, all healthy looking. They tell you that you are in a select group that is about to leave on a mission to find another planet to live on. Earth has become overcrowded, badly polluted, worn out, and dangerous. Wars, famine, and disease have made it unlivable. You don't really believe them, but they seem serious.

Then a large spacecraft arrives. You all get aboard and accelerate into space. It's all too familiar to you. This is the way you started, on a spaceship going between galaxies. It's starting all over again. Will the adventures never end?

The End

So, Earth was too much for you. Wanted to escape, didn't you? Where to now? What planet can you go to? What galaxy? What time? The choice is yours. Maybe back to the beginning.

The End

A cleaning operation is exactly that. Once you have found no evidence of living creatures about, several small transporter ships are equipped with laser-spreading devices that will cleanse the area of any and all bacterial life. It is a drastic step, because the laser will eradicate all life forms. But, the operation has been ordered. You have no choice but to carry it out.

The End

The past is often rich with knowledge and solutions that the present has chosen to forget. You scan the data banks of the ship's computers for similar incidents. There have been similar plagues, and you discover a supposed cure. It was used on a remote planet, which was mostly desert, but with rivers and high mountains cutting into the wastelands of sand. It requires the sacrifice of ten percent of the population. Supposedly, the sacrifice will appease angry gods. Of course the Axlians won't go along with it. Who would?

There is no cure. The fever will have to run its course.

The End

How do you try to convince people to stop polluting their planet when they have been doing it for so long?

Maybe it's a hopeless task.

The End

You and your team members are transported back to the research ship to report.

"We are convinced that the Galactic Court under the Universe Governing Body should send a police team in to force reform on Axle."

"Easier said than done. That's interfering with the rights of an independent planet. How can we tell them how to live? They are only hurting themselves."

Your report and recommendation is sent to the Galactic Court. The court is sympathetic, but they say that there is nothing they can or will do. Axle will have to deal with its own problems.

The End

Incredible! Unbelievable! The Universe Governing Body has sent police forces in patrol ships to Axle. You and your research station are forced to land and made to join the Axlians in a permanent quarantine. There is no cure!

The End

Amazing! Incredible! The sight that meets your eyes on Axle is a wonder. The people are better. The fever has broken. The civilization is once again on the move. They welcome you with great happiness. Oddly, the cure for the fever is simple— complete rest in the light of the three moons of Axle for three weeks with no solid food and only moderate liquids. Simple, ancient, and effective. You are cured, and the future lies before you.

The End

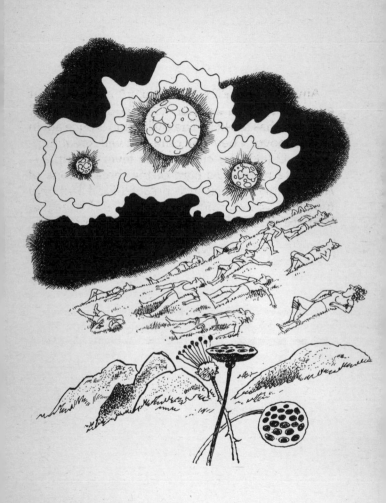

ABOUT THE AUTHOR
AND ILLUSTRATOR

R. A. Montgomery is an educator and publisher. A graduate of Williams College, he also studied in graduate programs at Yale University and New York University. After serving in a variety of administrative capacities at Williston Academy and Columbia University, he co-founded the Waitsfield Summer School in 1965. Following that, Montgomery helped found a research and development firm specializing in the development of educational programs. He worked for several years as a consultant to the Peace Corps in Washington, D.C. and West Africa. For the last five years, he has been both a writer and a publisher.

A graduate of Pratt Institute, *Paul Granger* is a prizewinning illustrator and painter. Mr. Montgomery and Mr. Granger previously collaborated on *Journey Under the Sea* in the Choose Your Own Adventure Series.